Holiday spirit was in the air . . . and on the floor!

Miss Mackle turned the page and rocked in her chair.

Krikkity krikk.

Krikkity krekk.

". . . not a creature was stirring, not even a—aaaaaaaugh!"

Suddenly the creaky chair tipped all the way back and the bottom fell through!

Miss Mackle landed on the floor with a THUD! *and* KABOOM!

"MY GOODNESS GRACIOUS!" she shouted.

There was our teacher, sitting on the floor, on broken pieces of wood!

BOOKS ABOUT
HORRIBLE HARRY AND SONG LEE

Horrible Harry
and the
Christmas
Surprise

BY SUZY KLINE
Pictures by Frank Remkiewicz

PUFFIN BOOKS

PUFFIN BOOKS
Published by the Penguin Group
Penguin Putnam Inc., 375 Hudson Street, New York, New York 10014, U.S.A.
Penguin Books Ltd, 27 Wrights Lane, London W8 5TZ, England
Penguin Books Australia Ltd, Ringwood, Victoria, Australia
Penguin Books Canada Ltd, 10 Alcorn Avenue, Toronto, Ontario, Canada M4V 3B2
Penguin Books (N.Z.) Ltd, 182-190 Wairau Road, Auckland 10, New Zealand

Penguin Books Ltd, Registered Offices: Harmondsworth, Middlesex, England

First published in the United States of America by Viking Penguin,
a division of Penguin Books USA Inc., 1991
Published in Puffin Books, 1993
Reissued 1998

20 19 18

THE LIBRARY OF CONGRESS HAS CATALOGED THE PREVIOUS PUFFIN EDITION AS FOLLOWS:
Kline, Suzy.
Horrible Harry and the Christmas Surprise / by Suzy Kline;
pictures by Frank Remkiewicz. p. cm.
"First published in the United States of America by Viking Penguin,
a division of Penguin Books USA Inc., 1991"—T.p. verso.
Summary: When their teacher ends up in the hospital, the members of
class 2B find a way to include her in their holiday celebration.
ISBN 0-14-034452-7
[1. Schools—Fiction. 2. Christmas—Fiction.]
I. Remkiewicz, Frank, ill. II. Title.
PZ7.K6797Hnj 1993
[Fic]—dc20 93-15137 CIP AC

This edition ISBN 0-14-130145-7

Printed in the United States of America

RL: 2.4

Here's to more
happy times at
Southwest School

Contents

Horrible Sounds

*K*rikkity krikk.
Krikkity krekk.

The teacher rocked back and forth in her old reading chair.

Harry leaned on his elbow and made a wide smile. I could see his pink gums where his two front teeth used to be. "Don't you love that sound, Doug?"

Krikkity krikk.
Krikkity krekk.

"No," I said, shaking my head. But Harry would. He loves things like that... slimy things, creepy things, hairy things, and *horrible sounds*. I know. I sit next to him in Room 2B. Harry's my best friend. Even his cat's name has a horrible sound—Googer. Sometimes he just calls him "The Goog," which sounds kind of scary.

Suddenly a fire truck zoomed by South School sounding its siren.

DEE doo, DEE doo, DEE doo.

Harry jumped out of his seat and ran to the window. "Look! There it goes, speeding in the snow!"

"Harry!" Miss Mackle called. "Sit down."

DEE doo, DEE doo, DEE doo.

Harry watched the fire truck zoom up and over the hill. Then he sat down, folded his hands, and gave the teacher a gummy smile.

"I think we're ready now for a story," Miss Mackle said. "It's a very special story because it's been read over and over for 168 years!"

Sidney threw his hands in the air. "Why read it if everyone's read it so much?"

"Because it's so good, Sidney."

"If I've heard it, I don't want to hear it again," he said, plugging his ears.

"READ THE STORY!" the rest of us shouted.

Miss Mackle rocked in her chair as she opened her big, heavy storybook and turned to the right page.

" 'Twas the night before Christmas,

and all through the house . . ."

"I love that story," Mary exclaimed.

"Me, too!" Sidney said, taking his fingers out of his ears.

While everyone was clapping and cheering, Ida said, "Miss Mackle, you look pretty today in your green dress and green sparkly earrings."

Miss Mackle whispered "thank you" as she turned the page and rocked in her chair.

Krikkity krikk.

Krikkity krekk.

". . . not a creature was stirring, not even a—*aaaaaaaugh*!"

Suddenly the creaky chair tipped all the way back and the bottom fell through!

Miss Mackle landed on the floor with a *THUD!* and *KABOOM!*

"MY GOODNESS GRACIOUS!" she shouted.

There was our teacher, sitting on the floor, on broken pieces of wood!

The big heavy storybook went flying in the air! It knocked the globe off its stand, and sent the world bouncing into the hallway.

THUNK! THUNK! THUNK!

One of Miss Mackle's green sparkly earrings took a nosedive into the fish tank.

BLUB! BLUB! BLUB!

Three guppies took a quick look and then swam away fast!

Everyone got out of their seats and

rushed to the teacher. We stood there in a circle with our mouths open.

"Are you okay?" we all asked.

Miss Mackle started to giggle. "Well, I'm glad I fell gracefully. I could be standing on my head."

While the rest of the class was laughing, I covered my eyes.
I didn't want to
picture the teacher
standing on her head!

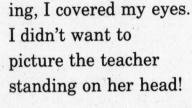

After we helped her get up, we took the wood pieces and dropped them in the big wastepaper basket.

CLUNK, BONG, THUNK!

"That was a dumb old rocker!" Sidney said, slapping his hands clean.

"No, it wasn't," Harry replied. "I liked that krikkity old chair."

"*You* just like horrible things!" Sidney replied.

"*You* are just off your rocker!" Harry said, holding up a fist.

"Now! Now!" Miss Mackle said, limping back to her desk chair. "Christmas is only four days away. It's time for peace and goodwill."

Just then the principal showed up at the door. "Anybody in here need a world?" he asked, holding up the globe.

"We do!" Miss Mackle exclaimed. Everyone laughed as the principal returned the world to the globe stand.

"Miss Mackle, are you going to finish the story?" Mary asked.

"What story is Miss Mackle reading?" Mr. Cardini asked.

The Night Before Christmas," Mary replied. "It's 168 years old."

"That old, huh? Well, I haven't heard it yet this year! May I join you?" he said, pulling up a little blue chair from the library table.

"What do you think, class?" Miss Mackle asked.

"YEAAAAAASSSSSS!"

Miss Mackle opened her big heavy storybook and turned to the right page. "Why doesn't everyone help me read the story this time!"

Everyone sat up and waited for their cue.

" 'Twas the night before . . ."

"Christmas!" we called out.

"And all through the . . ."

"House," Mr. Cardini boomed.

"Not a creature was . . ."

"Stirring," we replied. Harry made monster hands.

"Not even a . . ."

"Mouse!" Mr. Cardini twisted his moustache and squeaked.

Song Lee giggled.

Sidney laughed so hard he was snorting like a pig.

Room 2B is full of sounds. Some of them are horrible, and some of them are fun.

11

Mr. Cardini
Takes Over

When Harry and I got to the class-room the next morning, Miss Mackle wasn't at her desk.

"Where is she?" we asked.

Mary looked at the fish tank. "She's not putting in a new filter."

Ida looked at the science table. "She's

not making sugar water for the ant monitor."

Song Lee looked at the plant corner. "She's not putting a bug in the terrarium for the Venus's-flytrap."

Harry looked at the drama corner. "She's not trying on her Mother Goose costume for our Christmas skit."

"She's not changing the clothespins on our monitor chart," Sidney said.

"WHERE IS MISS MACKLE?" the class asked.

I held up a finger. "I'll go down the hall and see if she's still having coffee with the teachers in the teachers' room. The late bell hasn't rung yet."

"I'll go with you," Harry said.

As we walked down the hall, we saw the first-graders and kindergartners hanging up their winter jackets, and

putting their caps and mittens carefully in their jacket sleeves.

The kindergarten teacher was standing by the door with her hands behind her back. "Hello, Harry and Doug. We're looking forward to your skit this afternoon, 'Merry Christmas from Mother Goose.'"

Harry and I smiled at Mrs. Chan. We had her in kindergarten.

"What happened to your teeth, Harry?" she asked.

Harry showed off his pink gums. "I rammed into a wall."

Mrs. Chan took a closer look. "Hmmmmm. I also see some new ones coming in!"

Harry nodded. He was happy about that. "Did you see Miss Mackle?" he asked.

"No, I didn't. I've been mixing fin-gerpaint all morning." Then she wig-gled her red gooey hands at us! "We're painting Santa Clauses today!"

Harry and I took a big step back. "Let's get out of here!" I said.

When we got to the teachers' room, we knocked.

Mrs. Michaelsen, the librarian, opened the door. We could smell coffee and something buttery. "Good morning, boys," she said. "What can I do for you?"

Harry drooled when he saw the tray of frosted Christmas cookies on the table. I liked the big computer printout that hung from the lights. MERRY CHRISTMAS! HAPPY HANUKKAH! JOY TO ALL!

"We're looking for Miss Mackle," I said.

"She's usually in her room by now. Go back and check. Maybe her car stalled. It was 15 degrees this morning!"

We rushed back down the hall and into the classroom just as the final bell rang.

Mr. Cardini was standing in front of the class. He was not smiling. Harry and I wondered if we were in trouble. Quickly, we rushed to our seats.

"Boys and girls," he said. "I have some bad news."

Room 2B was pin-quiet.

"Miss Mackle went to the emergency room early this morning about her knee. Remember how she fell yesterday?"

Everyone nodded their head slowly.

"She thought she would just get it checked and then limp back to class. She didn't want to miss all the special activities you had planned.

"Well, when the doctor had her knee X-rayed, he discovered she had torn a ligament. She's going to need special surgery and was just admitted to the hospital. She called me as soon as she could."

Everyone groaned, "The hospital!"

I noticed Harry wiped his eyes with

his sweater sleeve. I think he was trying not to cry. "When will she be back?" he asked.

"After Christmas vacation, Harry. And then, she'll be teaching in a wheelchair for a while."

"Oh . . ." Sidney grumbled, "we won't be able to do our Christmas skit."

Harry leaned over the aisle and put a fist next to Sidney's nose. "Who cares about the skits? Our teacher is in the hospital!"

"Wait a minute," Mr. Cardini said. "Why can't you still give your skits?"

"We don't have a teacher!" Mary complained.

"Yes, you do."

"WHO?" we all asked.

"Me."

"But you're the principal!" I said.

"Most principals were teachers before they became principals."

"They were?" Sidney made a face.

"Yes. And sometimes when a principal can't get a substitute at the last minute, he has to take over a teacher's classroom."

Sidney pounded his fist on the desk. "We're doomed," he whispered. "We have Mr. Cardini for a teacher."

"No, we're not!" I whispered back. "Remember when I put mousse on his head in my demonstration talk? He liked his hair spiked. Mr. Cardini is a cool guy."

"But who would play Miss Mackle's part in our Christmas skit today?" Mary moaned.

"I can!" Mr. Cardini said.

We all laughed. Sidney snorted like a pig.

"What's so funny? What part do I have to play?"

"MOTHER GOOSE!" we shouted.

Mr. Cardini fiddled with his moustache. "I can do Mother Goose. Where's her costume?"

Mary ran to get it in the costume box in the drama corner. "Song Lee's mother made it."

We all stared at the principal as he put the elastic skirt over his head, then the blouse with the big collar, and then the flowered apron.

"Song Lee, come up and tie this for me, please."

Song Lee got out of her seat and made a nice bow. "You need the bonnet," she said softly. And she went back to the costume box.

When Mr. Cardini put the white bonnet on his head, we all laughed again!

"I never knew Mother Goose had a moustache!" Sidney cackled.

"Okay, boys and girls, the show will go on."

Everyone cheered except Harry. He had his head down on his desk.

Mr. Cardini went over to him and patted his back. "Are you feeling horrible, Harry?"

24

Harry nodded. He didn't like *this* kind of horrible. "I don't feel like being Georgie Porgie. Miss Mackle is in the hospital. I just want to be sad."

"Well, I know it would make your teacher sad if her accident kept you from doing your Mother Goose skits."

"It would?" Harry put his head up.

"Yes. She would want you to give them as planned for the kindergarten and first-grade classes."

"Could we dedicate our performance to our teacher?" Harry said, wiping his eyes again with his sleeve.

"I'll let you make the announcement before the skit begins. Okay, Georgie Porgie?"

Harry sat up and smiled. Then he lowered his thick eyebrows. I knew he had just gotten an idea. "Can we videotape it for Miss Mackle?"

"That's a great idea, Harry," Mr. Cardini said. "Mrs. Michaelsen has a camera. Let's ask her."

"YIPPEE!" we cheered.

After lunch everyone went to get their costumes. Harry put his thumbs in his ears and wiggled his fingers. "GIRLS BEWARE! Georgie Porgie is ready to *get* you!"

Mary, Ida, and Song Lee put their hands over their eyes. Harry had the horrible part of trying to kiss the girls and make them cry.

Mr. Cardini rolled his eyes. I think he was beginning to learn that there are two kinds of horrible.

"AAAAAUUUGH!" Mary screamed.

"HELP!" Ida shrieked.

Harry was chasing Song Lee, Mary, and Ida around the room.

"GEORGIE PORGIE IS TRYING TO KISS US!" the girls yelled.

Harry Stays After School

*T*ick tock.

Tick tock.

Harry sat with his hands folded on his desk while the classroom clock ticked loudly. It was 3:15. I was finishing my get-well card to Miss Mackle at the library table.

"Are you about finished, Doug?" Mr.

Cardini asked. "I want to take the letters and the videotape of our skit up to the hospital."

"I just need to color in my Indian's headband. I gave him 15 feathers."

"You're putting an Indian on Miss Mackle's get-well card?"

"Well, sometimes the Indians didn't have a very good Christmas. It was cold and there wasn't always enough food. I just thought it would make Miss Mackle feel better if she knew the Indians had hard times, too."

"Good thinking, Doug. There's a saying for that—misery likes company."

Mr. Cardini got up from his desk, and walked over to Harry's.

It was pin-quiet again. The second hand on the clock seemed louder than usual.

TICK TOCK.

TICK TOCK.

It wasn't a happy sound.

"You know why I am keeping you after school?"

"I chased too many girls?"

"Right. You overdid it, Harry. You started chasing girls at noon recess. The aides complained to me about it."

"I was practicing my part for Georgie Porgie."

"You were suppose to PANTOMIME ONE KISS, like this . . ." Mr. Cardini made fish lips and a funny puckering sound. *"SmmmmmmACK!"*

"I guess I got carried away."

"Yes, you did. You actually kissed Song Lee on the cheek."

31

Harry flashed his pink gums, and made his bushy eyebrows go up and down. I could tell he was thinking about his scene with Song Lee.

"It's *not* funny, young man."

I colored hard on my get-well card. I didn't want Mr. Cardini to think I was listening.

"So, I want you to write a letter of apology to Song Lee, and say that it will NEVER happen again."

"Yes, sir."

"Do you have anything to say to me?"

"I'm sorry, Mr. Cardini. It won't happen again."

"Good."

"I'm finished, Mr. Cardini," I said, handing him the get-well card.

"How colorful! I'm sure Miss Mackle will be very pleased."

"Can we visit Miss Mackle at the hospital?" I asked.

"No, Doug. You are not an adult. Only adults are allowed on the fourth floor. I'm sorry."

I made a face. It wasn't fair.

When I looked over at Harry he was busy writing. "I'll wait for you outside," I said.

Harry jumped out of his seat. "I'm done!"

Mr. Cardini looked at the letter as he pulled on his moustache.

Dear Song Lee,

I didn't meen to kiss you on the cheek in the class skit. I ment to pan toe mime. You were so pritty as Little Miss Muffit I jus forgot But it wont happen agen

Love forevr

Harry

"You'll have to change the last part. It's a little strong," Mr. Cardini said, trying not to smile. " 'From', or 'sincerely' is better."

Harry took out his *Tyrannosaurus rex* eraser and started erasing so hard he made a hole in his paper. When Mr. Cardini blew the ends of his moustache up, I knew he was trying to keep his temper down.

"There," Harry said, handing him back the paper.

Dear Song Lee,

I didn't meen to kiss you on the cheek in the class skit. I ment to pan toe mime. You were so pritty as Little Miss Muffit I Jus forgot But it won't happen agen

Sinseerlee
Harry

"Okay, Harry. You can go," the principal said. "But I expect very good behavior tomorrow. It's the last day before vacation. I want it to be a happy day, not a horrible day. Is that clear?"

Harry nodded as he listened.

"Miss Mackle won't be happy when she finds out you had to stay after school."

"You're going to tell *her?*" Harry's eyebrows shot up high.

"I have to report the whole day."

Harry's eyebrows sank down low. I could tell he was working on an idea.

When we were walking home in the snow together, Harry said, "Last Christmas my grandfather was in the hospital. I felt bad. My mom let me make him a gift and put it under the tall Christmas tree in the hospital lobby. They have someone dressed up like Santa Claus who delivers the gifts to the patients on Christmas morning."

"Neato!" I said.

"So, I'm making Miss Mackle a gift and taking it to the hospital tomorrow after school."

I put my arm around Harry as we stomped and squished some snow with our boots.

CRUSH! CRUNCH!
CRUSH! CRUNCH!

When Harry *knows* he's been bad, he tries to make up for it by being good.

The Horrible Christmas Gift

"Jingle Bells!
Jingle Bells!
Jingle all the way . . ." Mr. Cardini was singing by the record player as we walked into class.

"I love the way your mother fixed your hair!" Mary exclaimed.

"Thank you," Song Lee replied. "We wear hair like this in Korea for happy occasion."

"Do you celebrate Christmas in Korea?" Mary asked.

"Many people do. We have a big family feast. Many relatives come and we eat many dish of food."

"What is your favorite?" I asked.

Song Lee grinned. "Mandduguk."

"What's that?" we asked.

"Meatball soup."

"Mmmmmm," Harry and I said.

"*Blaaaaaugh*," Sidney groaned, falling on the floor and rolling over dead.

We all stepped over him except Harry. Harry stepped on Sidney's behind.

"OUCH!"

"He's not dead," Harry said.

"Let's go see what Ida is doing," Mary said.

Everyone walked over to the writing corner. Ida was tapping her pencil and humming something. "I got it!" she exclaimed.

"Got what?" we asked.

"I just made up a song we can sing to Miss Mackle after school."

"We can't visit her," I said. "Mr. Cardini told me so. You have to be an adult."

"I know that!" Ida said, standing up. She waved her paper in the air. "We can sing this outside her hospital window."

"Like carolers!" Mary exclaimed.

Mr. Cardini walked over and examined the refreshment table. "Look at all these goodies! Marshmallow Santas,

candy canes, cheese and crackers with olive and pimiento happy faces, frosted cookies, fortune cookies, whoopie pies! *Mama mia! Magnifico!*"

Everyone laughed. Sometimes Mr. Cardini spoke in Italian.

We went up to the principal as he admired the challah bread.

"Mom braided that," Mary said proudly. "She braids bread just like she braids my hair."

"Ah!" the principal replied. "Exquisite!"

"Mr. Cardini," Ida said. "Could you Xerox the words of my song? Some of us who live near the hospital want to go and sing it outside Miss Mackle's hospital window after school."

The principal quickly read Ida's lyrics. *"Bravo! Bravissimo!"*

"MR. CARDINI!" we replied.

"Okay," he said pulling on his moustache. "I'll ask our secretary, Mrs. Foxworth, to do it right away."

When the girls returned to their seats, Harry started talking about his gift.

"You're giving Miss Mackle a gift?" Mary asked.

Harry nodded.

"Did you wrap it?"

Harry shook his head.

"Did it cost very much?"

Harry shook his head.

"What is it?"

Harry shook his head again. Then he flashed his pink gums. "It's a surprise."

"Well, what does it look like?"

Harry thought for a moment. "It has ants on it, and spiders on it . . ."

"HARRY! THAT'S A HORRIBLE GIFT!" Ida and Mary exclaimed.

"The teacher will love it," Harry replied.

"She'll *hate* it!" Mary said. "You can't give Miss Mackle a horrible gift. It's sad enough she has to spend Christmas morning in the hospital. She doesn't need a horrible gift from you, too!"

"I'm putting my gift for Miss Mackle

underneath the Christmas tree at the hospital after school whether you like it or not."

Harry pulled out his library book and started reading about *Tyrannosaurus rex*. Everyone knew he wasn't going to talk about it anymore.

Mary did at recess. The girls met by the dumpster.

"We have to stop him," Mary said.

"How?" Ida asked.

"As soon as he puts his horrible gift under the tree, we wait behind a bush. We'll tiptoe into the lobby and get his gift."

"How will we know which one?" Ida asked.

"His gift isn't wrapped, remember?"
Ida remembered.

"It will be the only horrible gift under the tree. I'll bring a big bag and we can stash it in there. When we're caroling, he'll never know his gift is in my bag."

Mary got Sidney to join their scheme, too. He was angry with Harry for stepping on his behind.

I was sticking with Harry. When we stopped by his house to pick up the gift, boy, was I surprised!

We carried it up the hill to the hospital, and into the lobby. Harry put it right next to the tree.

When we came out, the girls and Sidney were waiting for us.

"Before we start to sing for Miss Mackle, we want to see the hospital tree. It's supposed to have beautiful decorations."

"Heh! Heh! Heh!" I said. I knew what they were doing. They were spying on

Harry's gift. They couldn't wait to take it away!

As soon as they got inside the lobby, they saw Harry's horrible gift. How could they miss it? It was big!

Mary's eyes bulged. "Oh, Harry, it's . . . wonderful!"

"I love it!" Ida said.

"You draw little ants and spiders on it so nicely!" Song Lee said.

49

"You even spelled my name right!" Sidney said proudly.

We all stared at Harry's gift.

It was an old wooden chair painted white. On the back he'd printed MISS

MACKLE'S READING CHAIR in bright red paint. On the seat was a message: BE-WARE: THIS IS FOR THE TEACHER ONLY!

Harry painted black ants and brown tarantulas crawling up and down the legs. Everyone's name in Room 2B was somewhere on the chair.

"Mom helped me with the spelling," Harry said.

"You were right, Harry," Mary said. "Miss Mackle will love your gift!"

"Let's go outside and sing my song," Ida said.

And we raced outside by the hospital building and got out our sheet music.

"Hmmmmmm." Mary hummed the right note for us.

"Remember," I said. "The words go to the tune of 'Jingle Bells.'"

We all nodded.

ROOM 2B
ROOM 2B
That's the place for me.
We read books
We're not snooks
And we write the best storie-ies!

Miss Mac-kle
Miss Mac-kle
We hope you hear our song.
Thanks for making class so neat,
In Room 2B we long . . . FOR . . .

Miss Mac-kle
Miss Mac-kle
Come back to us real soon.
You're the best
In the West,
So, here's to our dear Room . . .

"*2B!*" we shouted at the end.

"That's dumb," Sidney said. "We live in the East. How can she be the best teacher in the West?"

"It has to rhyme," Ida snapped.

"Who cares about the East or West! Where's Miss Mackle?" Harry complained.

We all looked up and groaned. No one saw Miss Mackle. While we were moaning some more, Harry screamed, "IT'S HER!" Quickly he wiped his eyes with his sleeve.

There on the fourth floor in front of the picture window was Miss Mackle. She was sitting in a wheelchair waving at us!

We all jumped up and down and waved back. "HI, MISS MACKLE!" we shouted.

Harry was so happy he stood on his head in the snow.

Mary hummed the note again. "Hmmmmmmmm."

And we all began to sing Ida's song.

The best sounds of Room 2B are the happy ones we make together.